The Shopping Expedition

André Amstutz

The Shopping Expedition

words by Allan Ahlberg

First published 2005 by Walker Books Ltd
87 Vauxhall Walk, London SE11 5HJ

This edition published 2006

10 9 8 7 6 5 4 3 2

This book has been typeset in FC Kennerly Regular

Printed in China

British Library Cataloguing in Publication Data:
a catalogue record for this book is available from the British Library

ISBN 978-1-4063-0123-6

www.walker.co.uk

WALKER BOOKS
AND SUBSIDIARIES
LONDON • BOSTON • SYDNEY • AUCKLAND

That was the day
that Mum and I
and little Harry
and Wilf the Wonderdog
went shopping.
Mum made her usual list:

...and off we went.

On the way the car broke down,

but we kept going.

The rain came down,

but we kept going.

The road got steeper ...

and steeper.

The *snow* came down, the wind blew up a blizzard

and Wilf the Wonderdog pulled us along.

The sun came out.

The road got narrower ...

and twistier ...

and greener.

But we kept going.

The *jungle* got thicker,

but we kept going.

Mum saved us
from the snakes.
Wilf saved us
from the crocodiles.
I saved us from the
cheeky monkeys.

The road became a river,

but we kept going.

The river became ...

a sea!

The sea rose and fell and washed
us to the shore.

Yes,
that was the day –
and the night –
that Mum and I
and little Harry
and Wilf the Wonderdog
went shopping ...

to the shop on
the shore.

And it was still ...

The End